cloverleaf books™

Alike and Different

My Home, Your Home

Lisa Bullard

illustrated by Paula Becker

M MILLBROOK PRESS • MINNEAPOLIS

For Grandpa T. —L.B.

To my father—for your ever-
constant love and support —P.B.

Millbrook Press
A division of Lerner Publishing Group, Inc.
241 First Avenue North
Minneapolis, MN 55401 USA

For reading levels and more information, look up this title at
www.lernerbooks.com.

Main body text set in Slappy Inline 18/28.
Typeface provided by T26.

Library of Congress Cataloging-in-Publication Data

Bullard, Lisa.
    My home, your home / Lisa Bullard ; illustrated by Paula
Becker.
       pages cm. — (Cloverleaf books™ — alike and different)
    Includes index.
    ISBN 978-1-4677-4904-6 (lib. bdg. : alk. paper)
    ISBN 978-1-4677-6032-4 (pbk.)
    ISBN 978-1-4677-6294-6 (EB pdf)
    1. Dwellings—Juvenile literature. I. Title.
GT172.B85 2015
392.3'6—dc23   2014023481

Manufactured in the United States of America
1 – BP – 12/31/14

TABLE OF CONTENTS

Chapter One

A Family Living Apart

Ahoy, there! I'm Jayden. Did you know "ahoy" is a way to call a ship? I know that because **my mom is in the navy.**

My mom is away on sea duty right now. That means she's living on a navy ship. I'm staying with Grandma and Grandpa until she comes back.

I love Grandma and Grandpa. But I can hardly wait to see Mom again. Mom says it will be soon. Then we'll find our own place to live together.

Mom asked me to be a good helper while she's gone. So I'm checking out the different places people live. That way I can help pick out the right home for my family.

Sometimes families live together. Sometimes they live apart. What members of your family live with you? What members live somewhere else?

Chapter Two

Different Homes

My cousins' apartment is high up in a tall building in the busy city. The building also has many other apartment units. That means my cousins have lots of friends to play with. **The moon seems really close when I'm up high like this.**

"An apartment building would be great," I tell Grandma when she picks me up. "But Mom likes to explore new places. So maybe we should just **move to the moon**." Grandma laughs.

My friend Valeria lives in a different kind of apartment. It's the second floor of a house. Her mom rents it from the family who lives on the first floor. "It's called a **duplex house**," Valeria explains.

The first-floor family has three friendly dogs. Valeria and I get to play with them in the yard. It gives me an idea. **Maybe my family could find a house with lots of animals too!**

Hee! Hee!

Sometimes families own their own home. Other times, they rent a home that belongs to someone else. They pay that person money to live there.

Joseph is on my basketball team. He tells me his family owns their house. And there's another house in his backyard too. It's Joseph's **treehouse!**

"Let's pretend your treehouse is a navy ship," I tell him. "We'll sail across an ocean of leaves." I bet Mom would like living in this kind of treehouse!

Some homes have a yard. Some homes share outdoor space with other families. Other homes don't have an outdoor space. What about your home?

Grandpa takes me to visit his friend. "**Morris lives in a mobile home**," says Grandpa. "It was built somewhere else and then moved to this community. It's stayed here since."

Grandpa tells me there are also homes that people can drive around. He calls them RVs. "They come in handy for vacations," he says.

"If I lived in an RV, I'd sleep outside the amusement park. I could be the first one on the rides every morning!" I tell him.

Chapter Three

Neighbors and Friends

Morris tells me he's the **checkers champion** of his neighborhood. "There's always a neighbor who's ready to let me win," he says.

He also tells me that wasn't true when he was my age. "My family lived in a farmhouse out in the country," Morris says. "Neighbors were far away. But **the horses made really good friends.**"

Homes in the city are often smaller and closer together. Homes outside the city are sometimes bigger and farther apart. How close is your nearest neighbor?

Tara is a new kid at school. Her family just moved to town. They're staying at a motel for now. **Motels are nice places to visit.** But Tara's family wants to find a home of their own.

My family has to move a lot too. That's part of being in the navy. I told Tara I would be her first friend in town. I know that **finding a friend makes moving a lot easier!**

Chapter Four

The Perfect Home

There are lots of different homes to think about. **Just like families, homes come in all shapes and sizes.** But one of my best ideas is close by.

Grandpa and Grandma live in a townhouse. That means there is another townhouse attached to it. We could be neighbors!

But I'll be happy with whatever Mom chooses. It will be the perfect home, **because we'll live there together!**

FOR SALE

Plan Your Amazing Bedroom

If you could have any kind of bedroom, what would it be like? Use your imagination and go wild! Maybe your bed would be in a rocket ship zooming through the sky. Maybe you would curl up in a roller coaster car to dream sweet dreams. Or perhaps you'd sleep in a submarine deep down in the sea. Draw a picture of your make-believe bedroom.

Here are some things to think about:

1) Where will you sleep?

2) Where will you store your clothes and toys?

3) Will you share your room with someone else?

GLOSSARY

ahoy: used to call out to a passing ship or boat

apartment: a home inside a larger building

duplex house: a house containing two separate apartments

mobile home: a home built in a factory and then moved to a location where it often stays permanently

motel: a place where people stay for a short period of time, such as during a vacation or when moving to a new place

navy: part of a nation's armed services that fights at sea

rent: to pay someone in exchange for living in a home that they own

RV: a recreational vehicle, such as a camper or a motor home, used for traveling and camping

townhouse: a house attached to a similar house or houses through shared walls

BOOKS

Laroche, Giles. *If You Lived Here: Houses of the World.* New York: Houghton Mifflin Harcourt, 2011. See the amazing places people live in different parts of the world.

Moore, Max. *Homes around the World.* New York: DK, 2009. See pictures and read stories about some of the world's most unusual homes.

Shoulders, Michael. *The ABC Book of American Homes.* Watertown, MA: Charlesbridge, 2008. From apartment buildings to the White House, check out some of the places that Americans call home.

WEBSITES

PBS Kids Go!: When Your Family Moves: Can You Deal?
http://pbskids.org/itsmylife/family/moves/index.html
This website offers helpful advice about how to handle a family move, including how to say good-bye to one home and adjust to a new one.

Sadlier-Oxford: Homes around the World
http://www.sadlier-oxford.com/readers/socialstudies/book2/game.htm
Play a matching game with pictures of different homes around the world.

LERNER *e* SOURCE™
Expand learning beyond the printed book. Download free, complementary educational resources for this book from our website, www.lerneresource.com.